W9-BEF-963

STORIES OF THE STATES

GOLDEN QUEST

by Bonnie Bader

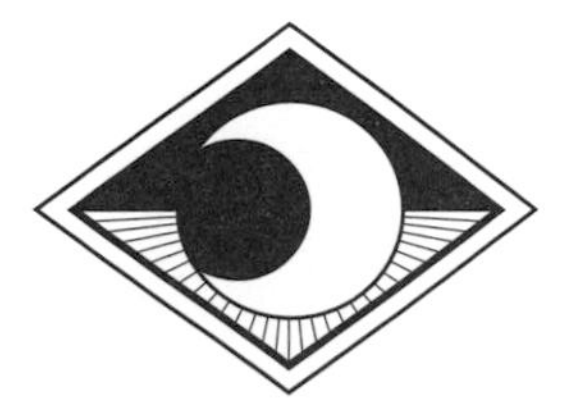

Silver Moon Press

New York

For information contact
Silver Moon Press
126 Fifth Avenue, Suite 803
New York, New York 10011

Distributed to the trade by
August House
PO Box 3223
Little Rock, Arkansas 72203

The publisher would like to thank JoAnn Levy, Woodland Hills, California, and Susan L. Johnson, The University of Michigan, for their help in preparing this book.

First Edition.

Cover Illustration by Nan Golub

Designed by John J. H. Kim

Printed in the United States of America

Library of Congress Cataloging-in-Publication Data

ISBN: 1-881889-30-0

CHAPTER ONE
"Caught in the Brawl"

"Come and get it!" Eleven-year-old David Taylor stepped aside as sixty men ran into the dining hall, each scrambling for a seat. They pushed and shoved each other for the chance to get a place at one of the long wooden tables. David and his younger sister Celia stood in the corner, making sure they were out of the stampede's path.

"Instead of calling this the gold rush, they should call it the food rush," David said to Celia, shaking his head.

As soon as the last seat was taken, David's mother closed the heavy wooden doors to the dining room. The men who didn't make it in would have to wait in the saloon for the next shift.

David wiped his hands on his food-stained apron. "Time to get to work," he grumbled.

He walked to the back of the dining hall toward the kitchen. Through a window, David could see his father bending over the stove.

"Hurry up, son," Mr. Taylor called. "Let's get the food out while it's still hot." Mr. Taylor wiped the sweat from his brow with a handkerchief and passed a large platter piled high with boiled beef and potatoes through the window.

David carefully carried the platter over to one of the tables.

"Hurry up, boy." A pair of rough hands grabbed the platter. "We're hungry!"

David stepped back from the table. He brushed his blond hair away from his eyes, slowly drew in a big breath, and listened to the clanking of the silverware against the plates. David's parents served two meals a day to the men in the mining camp who did not do their own cooking.

"David!" a man called. "Are you hard of hearing?"

David snapped to attention. "Sorry, Mr. Johnson," David said. Caleb Johnson was the *alcade* for the region. There was no government in the mining camp. As *alcade*, Johnson was the only person responsible for keeping law and order in the area. Johnson often ate at the dining hall. He bragged that Mr. Taylor cooked the best food in all of California. But David suspected that the Mr. Johnson also wanted to keep order at the dining hall and saloon.

"We're parched, son," Caleb Johnson told David.

David turned to fetch the water pitcher.

"Heard you found a bit of gold today, Wild Willie," Johnson said, as David bent over the table and poured water into the men's cups.

"Sure did," Wild Willie said, stuffing a piece of bread

into his mouth. "Staked out the spot, and found me a couple of big nuggets. Soon I'll be richer than you, Red," he said, digging his elbow into the ribs of the man next to him.

"Mrs. Taylor!" Wild Willie called. "I have some nuggets for you to store in the bank." Mrs. Taylor served as a banker for the miners. They trusted her to keep their gold safe.

"And tomorrow I'll have some for you," Red said. His bushy red beard bobbed up and down as he spoke.

David loved to listen to the gold miners' stories. He wished more than anything that he could be out there in the beautiful wilderness, searching for gold. Instead, he spent his days in a dusty dining hall, feeding and cleaning up after a bunch of dirty men.

"Wake up, David." Celia poked her brother in the arm. "Dreaming about gold again?"

David looked at his sister. She was pretty smart for an eight-year-old. Somehow, she always seemed to know what he was thinking.

David nodded. "I can't help it. Why do I have to be here?" He kicked the dirt floor with his foot. "Why did Father open up this stupid saloon, anyway?"

Celia put her hands on her hips. "Not everyone can be a gold miner," she said. "Father tried looking for gold, and maybe it's just as well he didn't find any. The miners need a place to eat and drink." She looked out at the men in the dining hall. "Why, I bet we're richer than most of these men."

"I know, I know." David smacked his fist into his hand. "I only wish. . . ."

David's words were cut short by shouting from the other side of the room. David looked up. Oh, no, he thought. A fight. David ran over to see what was going on.

"A free state?" A man was shouting. "California will never be admitted to the Union if it's a free state. The folks in the states who own slaves will never allow it."

"You're wrong, Tex. The U.S. Senate already voted to admit California as a free state," a man named Ben said. "And now the House of Representatives will vote the same way, and old Rough and Ready—President Zachary Taylor—will sign that bill into law!"

"If the idiots in Washington D.C. let another free state in, they're bigger fools than I thought," Tex insisted, pounding his fist on the table. "Why, they might even make us free our slaves."

"That's right! Freedom is a right every man should have, and you know it!" Ben shouted.

Celia tried to drag David away. "The last thing we want to do is get caught in the middle of a brawl," she whispered.

"Leave me alone," David told his sister. He moved closer to Tex and Ben as they squared off.

"If you don't like it, you should take your slaves and leave California!" Ben yelled, jabbing a finger in Tex's chest.

"Don't you go on telling me what to do!" Tex snarled. He grabbed the collar of Ben's flannel shirt, and threw him back.

"Fellas! Fellas!" drawled a warm voice. David turned and saw Caleb Johnson walk over to the quarrelling men. He had a friendly smile on his face. "Let's be reasonable here," the *alcade* said.

"Butt out, Johnson," Tex said, wheeling around and sneering at the *alcade*. "We all know which side you're on, Yankee Johnson."

David saw Ben recover his balance and grab a chair. He lifted it over his head while Tex's back was turned, and was about to bring it crashing down onto Tex's head.

"Stop!" David called, springing at Ben and grabbing the chair. David heard Celia scream as he and Ben fell in a heap. David rolled across the dusty floor. He struggled to get back on his feet, but was almost trampled as men rushed to help out either Ben or Tex. Caleb Johnson stepped between the two groups of men, trying to stop the fight from growing. David dived under a table for cover as Tex lifted a chair and swung it at Johnson's head.

"Gentlemen!" boomed a voice.

Tex froze, the chair inches from the back of Johnson's head. David looked up and saw a man approaching from the opposite side of the room. He was well dressed, wearing a black suit. His dark hair was long and curly, and his moustache turned up at the ends. "Gentlemen," the man said in a smooth voice. "Let us not brawl like common ruffians." He had a tiny smile frozen on his face.

David shuddered. He didn't like the way the man looked. David usually could tell a lot about people just from looking at their eyes. Although his mouth was smiling, this man had eyes that looked like the ocean on a stormy night. Waves of anger were ready to tumble out. David crawled out from under the table.

"Now apologize to the boy for the trouble you caused him," the man said to Ben.

David felt the heat rise in his face. All eyes in the dining hall were focused on him.

"But he jumped on me, Mr. Hill," Ben said.

"Do it!" Mr. Hill said with sudden ferocity.

"Sorry, boy," Ben mumbled.

"Now we can get back to our little discussion," Tex said, a nasty grin on his face.

David looked up and breathed a sigh of relief as he saw his father approach.

"I will have none of your politicking in my dining hall," Mr. Taylor said firmly. "Do you understand?"

"I agree with you, sir," Mr. Hill said in an oily voice. "All of this chatter spoils my meal." He turned to Tex. "Come along, Tex," he said. "Let's head back to camp."

"But—" Tex began.

"How many times have I told you?" Mr. Hill snapped. "Don't waste your breath talking about slavery." He turned and looked at Mr. Taylor with hard eyes. "You'll never change a Yankee's mind—at least, not with words."

With that, Hill led Tex out of the dining hall.

Caleb Johnson watched Mr. Hill leave. "That fellow is as mean as a rattlesnake," Johnson said.

"Meaner," David muttered.

"WERE YOU SCARED?" Celia asked David as they were wiping down the tables.

"No," David answered. "Just a little embarrassed."

"Children, you know we don't allow fighting in the dining hall," Mrs. Taylor said. "The next time you see something like that starting, I want you to get your father right away. Do you understand?"

"Yes, mother—but it made me mad to hear Tex say California should have slaves," David said.

"I know how you feel, David," Mrs. Taylor said. "Your father and I feel the same way. But some things are better left up to the law."

There was no law that said he had to work in a dining hall the rest of his life, David told himself, wringing out a rag into a bucket. David swore that he was going to succeed where his father had failed. He would find gold, no matter what.

CHAPTER TWO
"Dreaming About Gold"

David sat up. He rubbed his eyes, then shook the cobwebs from his head. He'd had the most wonderful dream.

David had dreamed of a cool mountain stream, under tall green trees and golden rays of sunshine. He had dreamed of diving into the fresh, cool water, and seeing. . . .

David's smile beamed. Yes, he had dreamed of gold! Quietly, David climbed down from his bunk bed.

He glanced out of the window. Stars were still twinkling in the deep blue sky. David took a flannel shirt from his chest of drawers and pulled it over his head. Next, he slipped on a pair of black wool trousers, and bent down and picked up his heavy boots. David tiptoed out of his bedroom and down four steps to the first floor. The faint aroma of fresh bread his mother had baked the night before still lingered in the air.

David heard heavy, steady breathing in the next room. He peered into the dining room where five miners were still asleep, wrapped up in woolen blankets. Some slept on the floor, others on wooden benches that lined the walls. David's father charged the men one dollar a night to sleep there. But David never liked to get too close to those men—they were unshaven and smelly.

David turned away from the snoring men, and went outside. He sat on the dewy ground and pulled on his boots. David looked at the brightening eastern sky. Dawn was on its way. He stood up and started on his morning chores. He wanted to get them finished early today. Once they were completed, he'd begin his search for gold.

David thought over everything he had to do. First he had to collect wood and start the fire in the stove. Then he had to fill the big pots with water, and put them on the stove. His mother would be serving breakfast soon. David knew he wouldn't be missed at breakfast, since it was the least busy meal of the day.

After his chores in the kitchen were through, his job was to deliver laundry. Mrs. Taylor washed clothes for those people in the mining camp who liked to stay clean. But a lot of the men in the camp wore the same clothes every day. No wonder they smell, David thought with a smile.

The sun was up by the time David finished his kitchen chores. The camp was quiet. David rummaged through the kitchen, looking for supplies he would need for panning. "This'll do," he said out loud, reaching for a frying pan.

"Other miners pan for gold. I'll 'fry' for gold!"

Next, he picked up a tin cup. When I return home, this will be filled with gold, he thought.

Once outside, David closed his eyes and inhaled the cool, crisp October air. He had to admit that living in California wasn't so bad. Sure, it wasn't Massachusetts, where he came from, but it had its advantages. David looked out at the Sierra Nevada Mountains that towered in the distance, purple in the early morning light. The mountains held tumbling rivers and rolling streams, with secret lakes hidden in the hills.

David slung the heavy bag of laundry over his shoulder and started down the road. Soon the town would come alive. Miners would roll out of bed and head over to the river to begin their day's work. But David would get there first.

Snap!

David stopped. He had heard a twig break under a boot behind him. David's heart raced. Could someone be following him? Maybe someone had seen him in the kitchen, figured out his plan, and was going to put a stop to it. Slowly, he turned around.

"Celia!" David gasped, relieved.

"I thought you could use this," she said, holding out a loaf of bread. The morning's first light was glinting off her golden curls.

"Why are you following me?" David asked.

"I thought you'd want some company," Celia answered.

Underneath her long gray wool dress she wore a pair of wrinkled black boots.

David shook his head. His little sister was always tagging along. "Get back to the hotel, Celia. I won't be gone long," he said.

Celia frowned. "Well, all right. But you'll wish I went with you."

David turned to leave, then stopped. He sighed. Celia was right. He had heard that it could be mighty lonely out in the hills. "Okay," he said, handing her the frying pan and the tin cup. "But let's hurry. I don't want to face any claim-jumpers." They walked down the street, past the houses that made up Spring Bar, their little mining town. David dropped off parcels of laundry as they went. Their home, which served as a combination hotel, restaurant, and saloon, was the only two-story building in the town. It was built of planks of wood, with a canvas roof.

The other buildings in the town had been hastily built. Some were constructed from calico cloth and pine boughs, others from wood and canvas. Many of the "buildings" were simple tents. Miners found them to be cheap and easy to build, and tents could be packed up easily when the miner decided to try his luck at another mining camp.

Towns around here were built as quickly as snowmen, David thought. And they melted away just as fast—as soon as the last glimmer of gold faded away.

The camp was stirring to life as David walked down the main street, dropping laundry outside of buildings as he passed. David walked by a large tent where a group of Chinese men lived. Two of the Chinese men stepped out of the tent and breathed deeply the early morning air. They nodded at David, then walked around to the back of the tent. David had heard that these Chinese miners had taken over claims where other miners had failed to find gold. The Chinese miners had more luck. Maybe it was because they got up earlier and worked harder than the others, David thought with a smile. He would have that kind of luck, too!

David and Celia passed the local store. A sign in the window read: Butter: $2 a pound; Bread: $2 a pound; Cheese: $6 a pound. David shook his head. Back in Massachusetts, those prices would be outrageous. But most goods had to be shipped from the East, and that was expensive. Once the merchandise arrived in California, it had to be carried to the mining camps by mule, wagon, and sometimes even by foot. Of course, the merchants made sure there was a big profit for themselves, too.

David and Celia soon reached the edge of town, and David broke a path to the river. They walked past tall pine and oak trees, and brilliantly colored leaves of poison oak. David's heart beat fast and his stomach did somersaults as they walked along the river bank. He just knew that this was going to be his lucky day.

After walking for about a half an hour, David stopped. They were at a point where the river ran through a deep gully. A steep embankment rose from the river to the path where they stood. It was covered with small trees and scrub bushes. David looked down at the river below. The water glistened, moving in rhythmic patterns. It seemed to be beckoning him, calling his name.

"This is the place," David announced.

"But how will we get down there?" Celia wanted to know. Boulders had tumbled to the river bank, and trees were tangled together, seeming to block any sort of path.

"Don't you see?" David said. "This is a perfect spot. We'll be able to squeeze our way down to the river. I'm sure no adult has tried panning here yet."

And David was right. Despite a few minor scrapes, they made it down to the river. Nothing broke the surface of the clear water but the smooth stones of the river bed. David knew that prospectors always left some sort of marker which let other people know that a site was off limits. But nothing was here. They had first claim to the spot.

"Now that we're here," Celia declared, "what do we do?"

David smiled as he rolled up his pants legs. "We find gold!" he said.

He stepped into the river and gasped. The cold water on his legs was like a slap in the face. Somehow, he'd thought the water would be warmer. But that didn't matter. Determined, David knelt down and scooped up a handful of gravel, and placed it in his frying pan.

"Now I have to add some water," he told his sister. David had watched other miners perform this task. Now he was on his own.

David put the water into the pan, and began to swish it around. Around and around the water and the sand went. "If there's any gold in this pan, it'll sink to the bottom along with the sludge, since the gold weighs more than the gravel," David explained. "I have to be careful not to let too much of the sludge spill out."

"But it looks like a lot of it is," Celia said.

"I know," David said, frustrated. "This takes practice."

David stayed in the water for almost an hour without any luck. Then Celia tried. She found no gold, either. David tried again. After more than two hours of panning, they had found not a trace of gold. His back was stiff and sore from stooping over, his fingers numb from the icy water. David was beginning to lose hope.

"I've had enough of this, Celia," David said glumly, shaking the pan. "After this batch, we're going home."

More water and sand splattered from David's pan, but no gold appeared in the bottom. "That's it, Celia," David said, stretching his weary limbs. "We're heading back. It's almost time for mother to give us our school lessons, anyway."

"We can come back here tomorrow," Celia said, picking up a handful of rocks. "Let's put these in the tin cup. Maybe they'll bring us luck."

David shrugged. They left their pan at the site, marking it as their own, and headed home.

Celia skipped along the road, swinging the tin cup in her hand. David couldn't understand why his sister was so happy. They had failed—just like so many other miners had failed.

Suddenly, a figure stepped out from behind a tree and blocked their path. The man was dressed in tattered clothes, his hair matted down against his pale face. He grabbed Celia by the arm.

"Hand it over," he demanded, pointing to the tin cup.

David looked into the man's eyes. They darted back and forth like ants running into a hill. David didn't like those eyes.

"But there's nothing in here except some rocks," Celia protested, putting the cup behind her back.

"I saw you young 'uns in the river. And I know what 'rocks' you have in there," the man said. "Gold!"

"Do what he says," David told his sister. He had heard stories of bandits coming down from the mountains and robbing miners of their gold. Now he knew the stories were true.

"Listen to the boy!" the man said, jerking Celia's arm.

"But there is no gold in here," Celia squealed in anger.

What is she doing? David thought in alarm. *This man is dangerous. He could have a gun. He could—*

Just then, the man's head jerked forward. David jumped back, startled, as the bandit sprawled at Celia's feet!

CHAPTER THREE
"A New Friend"

Celia looked at her brother. "Wh-what happened?" she asked in disbelief.

"Psst!"

David and Celia looked around.

"Psst!"

Where was that sound coming from? David looked high up in the pine trees. Nothing. He looked down the path. No one was there.

"Over here," an exasperated voice called. David focused his eyes past the fallen man. There, standing beside a tree, was a boy. He looked to be about David's age, with chocolate-brown skin, high cheekbones, and short black hair. David saw that he wore brown woolen pants, and a tattered white shirt. In the boy's hand was a slingshot.

"Quick, get over here!" the boy said. "Before he wakes up."

David grabbed Celia's hand and ran over to the boy.

"Slingshot Winston, at your service," the boy said with a smile.

"Slingshot?" Celia said, puzzled.

"Well, most people just call me Georgie," the boy said, slipping the slingshot under his shirt.

"Thanks for your help, Georgie," David said. "How did you know we were in trouble?"

"I heard voices and came over. When I saw that man grab the girl, I decided to take some action." Georgie turned to Celia. "One time I saw a group of three bandits here," he said. "They were each seven feet tall and had long fangs."

"Really?" Celia asked in awe.

David bit his lip to keep from laughing.

"It's the truth," Georgie said, his eyes growing wider. "And they were holding rifles and cannons. But I knocked their weapons away with my slingshot."

"You're so brave!" Celia was definitely impressed.

"Well, I just hope that man isn't hurt too bad," Georgie said.

David looked back at the man, who was beginning to stir. "I think he'll be okay," David said. "But I don't want to wait and find out!"

The three ran down the path until they were a safe distance away. David stopped and bent over, trying to catch his breath. "By the way," he said, taking in big gulps of air, "I'm David Taylor, and this is my sister Celia. We live over in the Taylor Hotel."

Georgie smiled. "I don't see many people here around my age."

"Neither do we," Celia said. "Where do you live, Georgie?"

"Come on, I'll show you." Georgie motioned for Celia and David to follow him. "It's time to bring the horses back anyway."

David was so wrapped up in all the excitement that he hadn't noticed the horses tied to a tree a few feet from where they stood. The horses were beautiful—one black as coal, with a white patch on its forehead, and the other chestnut brown.

"Oooh, what pretty horses!" Celia cried. "Do they belong to you?"

"No," Georgie said. "They belong to Mr. Hill. I don't own anything."

"Mr. Hill—but he owns slaves," David said. He saw a cloud pass over Georgie's face.

"Yes. I know he does," Georgie said quietly.

There was a moment of silence as David and Celia realized the truth. Georgie was enslaved by Mr. Hill.

"But—that's not fair!" Celia exploded. "Slavery is illegal in California. It's not right!" she added, stomping her foot.

Georgie looked away. David leaned against the tree. It made him sick to his stomach to think that Mr. Hill could claim to "own" a human being like Georgie.

Georgie untied the horses and led them down the path. "So, what were you two doing out here by yourselves?"

David bit his lip. He wondered if they could trust Georgie with their secret.

"We were panning for gold," Celia burst out proudly. David groaned.

"Gold!" Georgie said, surprised. "I've tried looking for gold, too, but never had any luck."

"Neither did we," David said, pushing a tree branch away from his face as they came into a clearing.

"Georgie! Georgie Winston!" a woman's voice called.

David and Celia saw a tall, thin, dark-skinned woman standing in front of a tent, tending a fire. Her dark hair was in braids, and her face looked like Georgie's. The woman was mixing something in a large pot. She stood up and wiped her hands on her long skirt.

"Georgie, I'm speaking to you," the woman said sharply.

"Yes, Mamma," Georgie said.

"Where have you been, son? You were supposed to be back here an hour ago!" the woman scolded.

"I'm sorry, Mamma," Georgie said. "But I ran into some trouble. These are my new friends." Georgie pointed to David and Celia. "David and Celia Taylor."

"Hello, children," Georgie's mother said.

"Hello, Mrs. Winston," David and Celia said together.

"Now, Georgie, I don't have time to listen to another one of your wild stories. I'm busy with dinner," Mrs. Winston said. "Hitch up those horses, and come back here right away. Understand?"

"Yes, Mamma," Georgie answered.

David and Celia followed Georgie past several canvas tents. "Mamma and I live there," Georgie said pointing to one of the tents.

David noticed that in addition to the tents there were two little shanties covered with branches, sticks, and scraps of wood. Another black woman went about her daily tasks. David guessed that she was a slave, too.

"How many people live here?" Celia wanted to know.

There was no answer. "Georgie?" Celia said. "Where did he go?"

David looked around. "I don't know. He was here a minute ago."

"Got you fooled!" David and Celia heard Georgie say. But as they looked around, they still couldn't see him.

"Maybe he climbed a tree," Celia suggested.

"You're not even warm!" Georgie called.

David and Celia walked toward the sound of Georgie's voice. They stopped in front of a very large wagon and looked inside. It was empty.

"Come on, Georgie," David said. "We give up. Where are you?"

"But you were so close!" Georgie cried, climbing out of the wagon.

"How did you get in there?" Celia asked. "It was empty a second ago."

"This is a special wagon," Georgie explained. "You think this is the bottom, but it's really not." He lifted up what looked to be the floor, and revealed a secret compartment as wide and long as the wagon itself. "Mr. Hill had it special-built. He's going to use it to carry his gold back to Texas, so that bandits won't be able to find the loot. It's a great place to hide."

David and Celia laughed. "Georgie, I was thinking," David said. "How would you like to join our mining group?"

"That's a great idea!" Celia said. "What do you say, Georgie?"

Georgie hitched the horses to a tree. "Well . . . What are you calling your mining site?"

"What are we calling it?" Celia asked, confused.

"Sure," Georgie said. "All of the big mining sites have names." He stroked his chin thoughtfully. "What do you think of 'Slingshot' as a name for the camp?"

"'Camp Slingshot'?" David thought it over. "I like it," he said.

"Me, too," Celia said.

"Then it's a deal," David said with a big smile, and the three shook hands.

"I'll have to rise mighty early to do all my work, though," Georgie said. "I must feed and groom the horses, scrape the mud off the men's boots, wipe down their tools, and do whatever else I'm told."

"That's a lot of chores," David agreed. "But we have chores, too. We don't start panning till about two hours after dawn."

"That gives me time," Georgie said. "All right. I'll be

there to help find the gold."

"We'll meet you at the spot you first saw us," David said. "Then we'll take you down to Camp Slingshot."

"Georgie!" A deep voice interrupted them.

David looked up and saw a group of four men holding picks, shovels, pans, and buckets. All of them were dark-skinned except one.

"Yes, Mr. Ewell," Georgie said, standing at attention.

"Boy, why you botherin' these children? Get to work!" the white man said harshly. He stared at David and Celia. David recognized him. It was Tex, the man who had tried to start a fight in the dining hall. "You're the Taylor children, aren't you?" he asked.

"Yes, sir," David said.

"Well?" Tex Ewell demanded, looking back at Georgie.

"We were just leaving, sir," David said hastily, taking Celia by the hand. They turned and David gasped. Mr. Hill sat on horseback a few feet away, watching them closely. He didn't say a word, but nodded slightly as David and Celia passed.

"That was Mr. Hill, wasn't it?" Celia asked when they were a safe distance away from the camp. "He was the one who broke up the fight last night."

"That's right, Celia," David said. He remembered Mr. Hill well. He was the man with the storm brewing in his eyes.

CHAPTER FOUR
"Then We Will Leave"

David tossed and turned in his bed. He couldn't fall asleep. His imagination was floating in the river, searching for gold. Would they have any luck tomorrow?

He kicked off his woolen blanket and jumped out of bed. Maybe I'll be able to sleep after I've gotten something to eat, he thought. David quietly crept down to the kitchen.

"You know how I feel, Martha," David heard his father say.

"But after all we've gained here, Charles. All we have. I couldn't leave," David's mother replied.

David stood perfectly still. His parents were in the kitchen talking in low tones. David strained his ears to hear what they were discussing.

"We both know it could happen, Martha. We need to be prepared. On August thirteenth, the Senate voted to admit California to the Union," Mr. Taylor said.

"As a free state," Mrs. Taylor stated.

"True. But the House of Representatives is to vote on it next. They might have decided not to let California into the Union at all. What's more, President Taylor died this summer. Even if Congress voted to let California into the Union, who knows if President Fillmore would sign the bill?"

"The waiting is awful," Mrs. Taylor said. "When will we know if California is a state?"

"Two months have passed since the Senate voted," Mr. Taylor said. "The decision must have been made by now. By my calculations, a ship should be arriving in San Francisco with the news any day now."

David knew that it took a very long time for them to get news. Ships left the east coast loaded with newspapers. Then they had to travel all the way around Cape Horn, at the tip of South America, in order to reach California. By the time California got them, newspapers from the East were already months old.

"And what if they decide to cut California in half?" Mrs. Taylor asked. "We would be in the free state."

David knew what his mother was talking about. He had read about this in the newspaper, the *Alta California*. Some people wanted to make California into two states. San Francisco and Sacramento would be in the northern state, without slaves, and Los Angeles and Santa Barbara would be in the southern state, with slaves.

"That proposal is ridiculous! It will never happen,"

David's father said. "There will be no further discussion on this subject. If the slave owners have their way, we will leave. Now I'm going upstairs to bed."

David heard the sound of his father's heavy footsteps. There was no way he could sneak back upstairs now.

"David!" Mr. Taylor said. "What are you doing here?"

David cast his eyes down. "I couldn't sleep," he answered.

"I suppose you heard what I said to your mother," Mr. Taylor said.

David nodded.

Mr. Taylor put his arm around David. "Come on, son. We need to have a talk."

Mr. Taylor led David into the kitchen. His mother was sitting on a bench, her face illuminated by a candle. As David and his father walked in, she looked up, wiping a tear from her eye.

"Martha," David's father started. "It seems as though David overheard some of our conversation. I think he's old enough for an explanation."

David's mother nodded. David walked over and sat down on the bench next to her. He rested his elbow on the wooden table. "You know that California isn't a state yet," Mr. Taylor began, pacing the floor.

David nodded. "And I also know that the California government asked to become a state, and it wants to ban slavery. But what does that have to do with us?"

"Everything," Mr. Taylor said. He stood in front of

David and looked him in the eyes. "I am an abolitionist, and I refuse to raise a family in a place where men enslave their brothers. If the slave-owning forces have their way here, we shall leave California."

David closed his eyes. It would be hard for them to move back East, but he respected his father and his views. Yet David knew the events would have an even stronger bearing on Georgie's life. He did not have the freedom to pick up and leave.

David looked up at his father. "There's something about all of this that I don't understand."

"What is it?" he asked.

"Well, if the people here in California voted last year to outlaw slavery, then why do some people around here still have slaves?"

Mr. Taylor looked very serious. "The slave owners who live here don't have much respect for the law. Most brought their slaves with them from other states and use them to work in the mines and to keep their camps. But once California has joined the United States the law will be stronger. The slave owners will have to listen."

"And if California doesn't become a state?" David asked, although he already knew the answer.

"Then we will leave," Mr. Taylor said. "Then we will leave."

HIS CONVERSATION WITH HIS PARENTS made it harder than ever for David to fall asleep. His father's words echoed in David's mind.

"Then we will leave."

Yes, David thought. But what about Georgie? He would not be able to leave.

David jumped down from his bed and walked over to the window. The stars were winking at him, as if they held some deep, dark secret. Did the stars know what had happened in the District of Columbia?

"Then we will leave."

The words pounded in David's brain. Never before had David realized how powerful four simple words could be.

"Then we will leave."

CHAPTER FIVE
"A Golden Day"

"Wake up, sleepy head." Something poked David in the ribs. He brushed it away and rolled over.

"Come on, David," the voice said. "Get up or we'll be late!"

David cracked open one eye. It was still dark. He reached a hand over the side of his bunk bed and touched something soft and fluffy. It felt like someone's hair. "Celia?" David asked sleepily.

"Who'd you think it was?" Celia demanded.

David yawned and sat up. "What time is it, anyway?"

"Time for you to get up and start your chores. You have a lot to do this morning," Celia said. "Don't forget, we have to meet Georgie two hours past dawn."

David looked at his sister. She was wearing a blue and black flannel shirt, a long grey wool skirt, and wrinkled black boots. She looked as though she had been up for hours.

"I got up early," Celia explained. "I've already collected the water and the wood. But I need your help starting the fire."

"Okay, okay," David said. "I'll be downstairs in a minute."

"I HOPE GEORGIE CAN MAKE IT," David said. He leaned against a tall pine tree and looked around.

"It sounded like he had a lot to do this morning," Celia said.

Thwack!

Something hit the tree trunk just above David's head. "What was that?" David cried, jumping away from the tree. He looked up. The blue sky was peeking out between the prickly pine needles.

Thwack!

David bent down and picked up a rock that had landed a few inches from his feet. "Georgie?" he called out.

"How did you guess?" Georgie appeared from behind a tree, a big smile on his face, and his slingshot in his hand.

"You could have hit us," Celia said, frowning.

"Don't worry," Georgie assured her, "I'm the best shot around. Come on!" he said. "Let's get to work!"

The three skidded down the river bank to the site David and Celia had found the day before. The frying pan was where they had left it.

"Welcome to Camp Slingshot," Celia announced.

Georgie smiled. "Not bad," he said, looking around.

"Guess we have the whole place to ourselves."

"I didn't have any luck yesterday," David said "I probably was doing it wrong. Do you know how to pan for gold, Georgie?" He lifted up his pan.

"Sure. I've seen it done a million times," Georgie said. "But Mr. Hill would never use a frying pan," he added with a laugh.

"That's all we have," David said with a shrug.

"What else could we use?" Celia asked.

"Mr. Hill and his men use a rocker," Georgie explained.

"What's that?" Celia asked.

"Well, it's sort of like a baby cradle," Georgie said. "It's a wooden box that's open at one end and closed at the other. And these things called riffles are nailed in the bottom to catch the gold."

"I think I know what you're talking about," David said, nodding. "The box is put on top of rockers, right?"

Georgie nodded. "And then you shovel gravel in and pour water through. At the same time, you rock the cradle. The water and gravel flow out, and the gold is left behind."

"Sounds good, but for now this is our rocker," David said, holding up the frying pan. He took a deep breath and waded into the water. "Yeow, that's cold!"

"Once we make our fortune in gold, we'll be able to buy a big rocker," Celia said, hitching up her skirt and jumping into the water.

David picked up a handful of gravel and put it into the pan. "When we're rich, we won't need a rocker."

Celia cupped her hands and placed more gravel and water into the pan as her brother swished it around. "What are you going to buy with your gold, David?" she asked.

"I'll buy a ship and I'll sail it around Cape Horn," David said.

"You'd go back East?" Celia asked.

"Only to pick up all my friends in Massachusetts and sail them back here," David said. He looked in the pan. No specks of gold had appeared. "Then I'd let them live in my beautiful mansion!"

"I'd buy a beautiful horse," Celia said. "Maybe even two. What would you buy, Georgie?" Celia asked.

Georgie kicked at the water.

"I'd buy myself," he answered softly.

David stopped swishing his pan. Suddenly, his own plans and dreams seemed silly. He looked in Georgie's eyes. They were filled with quiet determination. At that moment, David knew that they *had* to find gold.

"You're not going to get anything by just standing there," Georgie said to David. "Besides, I think you're spilling too much sludge. Let me give it a try."

David stood up and handed the pan to his friend.

Georgie knelt down, scooped up a handful of gravel, and placed it in the pan. Next, he added some water, and swished it around. All of the water spilled out, along with sand and gravel. Only the sludge from the river bed was left behind.

"I can't believe it!" Georgie shouted, shaking the pan.

David and Celia looked down. There, in the sludge,

shining like a ray of sunshine through the clouds, was gold!

"You did it, Georgie!" Celia shouted. She jumped up and down in the water, hitting her brother with an icy spray.

"I knew it! I knew I could do it!" David said.

Celia glared at him, hands on her hips.

"I mean, I knew *we* could do it," David said with a sheepish smile.

"You two sure picked a good place to prospect for gold," Georgie said.

"We'd better be careful with this gold," David said. "Don't forget what happened last time," he added, remembering the bandit who had attacked them.

"I'll be our banker," Celia announced. "Just like Mother. Give the gold to me, and I'll keep it in a safe place."

"Now you give it a try, David," Georgie said, holding out the pan. "Go slow. Make sure that not a lot of the sludge spills out."

Georgie's was advice was good. In a short while two gleaming gold nuggets, each about the size of a pea, appeared in the pan. When it was time to head home, the group had collected ten gold nuggets in all.

"This was a great day!" Georgie said as they climbed up the riverbank.

"We'll meet you here tomorrow, then?" David asked their new friend.

"I can't make it," Georgie said, shaking his head. "Tomorrow I leave for San Francisco. I might be gone for two weeks."

"Oh," David said. He had almost forgotten about the expedition. Every three months, a group of men from their mining camp and the surrounding area traveled to San Francisco to pick up supplies. This was to be their last trip before the rainy season began. Once the rain began, it would be impossible to travel far.

"Our father will be going, too," Celia told Georgie. "I better tell him to watch out for you and your slingshot," she added with a laugh.

David heard loud voices. His heart skipped a beat. Were they going to run into bandits again? He motioned for the others to be still. The voices grew louder, and a group of men came into the clearing. It was Mr. Hill and four others.

"Boy! What are you doin' here?" Tex Ewell shouted when he saw Georgie.

"I was fetching water," Georgie replied.

"With what? I don't see a bucket," Tex said sternly. "You're going to be sorry, boy. Now git!"

Georgie stole a look at David and Celia and ran off down the road. Tex and the others followed Georgie. Mr. Hill remained in the clearing, smiling at David and Celia. "Good morning, children," he said in a voice that made David's skin crawl.

David grabbed his sister's hand and turned away from Mr. Hill.

THE LAST DINNER SHIFT WAS OVER. David and his father were alone in the dining room, cleaning up after the men. "Are you ready for your trip to San Francisco?" David asked his father as he wiped down the tables.

"Yes," his father answered. "And I expect you to look after your mother and sister while I'm gone."

David looked at his feet. His boots were crusted with mud. "Well actually, I was going to ask you—"

"Yes?" his father said.

"I was going to ask if I could go along," David said. He put his hands behind his back and crossed his fingers.

"I don't know, son." His father shook his head. "It's a very long trip. We're going all the way to San Francisco this time—not just Sacramento City."

Sacramento City served as a river port where miners could go to pick up supplies. David knew that his father preferred to go all the way to San Francisco. He could buy less expensive supplies from the merchants there.

"It's not an easy journey," Mr. Taylor said. "First we ride to the American River, and then catch a launch to the Sacramento River. After that, we board a steamboat to San Francisco."

"But I could do it," David insisted.

Mr. Taylor sighed. "Go ask your mother."

David smiled and ran toward the kitchen. He knew the answer would be yes!

CHAPTER SIX
"A Free State"

"I've packed some rolls, and beans, and beef," David's mother told him, as they stood in front of Taylor Hotel. "Be sure to eat all of the meat tonight, otherwise it will spoil."

"Yes, Mother," David said. He tied his pack onto the back of his horse. All around him, men were preparing for the journey. He and his father were among the few men traveling on horseback. Mules were being packed with blankets and supplies.

"I'm so glad you haven't left yet!" Celia said breathlessly as she ran up to her brother. "Take my poncho. It will help keep you warm at night."

"Thanks, Celia." David took the brightly-colored woolen cape from his sister, and tossed it over the saddle.

"David! Helping your father pack?" David looked up and saw Georgie coming towards him, leading a pair of pack mules.

"No," David said. "I'm helping myself pack."

"You mean you're going along?" Georgie said. "That's great!"

"Now, David," Mrs. Taylor said. "Be sure to sleep near the campfire. There are wild animals roaming around in those mountains."

"Yes, Mother," David said.

"And don't forget to wear your woollies."

Georgie giggled.

"Mother." David blushed.

"I'm just worried about your health, that's all," Mrs. Taylor said. "But it looks like you have a friend to keep you company," she said, smiling at Georgie.

David had forgotten that his mother had never met Georgie. "Oh, yes. This is Georgie Winston. Georgie, this is my mother."

Before Georgie could respond, a harsh voice interrupted. "I'm sorry, Mrs. Taylor!" Mr. Hill called out. David watched as Mr. Hill rode his horse toward them. "Is this boy bothering you?" he asked, looking coldly at Georgie.

"Not at all, Mr. Hill," Mrs. Taylor answered.

Mr. Hill raised his eyebrows. "Well, you're here to work, boy, not talk. Understand?"

Georgie lowered his head. "Yes, sir."

"Attention, everyone!" Mr. Taylor called out. "We're ready to leave."

David joined in the cheer. They were off!

David yawned, rubbed his bottom, then stretched. He hadn't realized how grueling the ride would be. Now it was long past dusk, and most of the men sat around a campfire that sent off sprays of shimmering light. One by one the men yawned and turned in to sleep. David heard howling in the distance. The animals that ruled the night were beginning to stir.

David tossed a stick into the fire. "This has been fun," he said. David watched as the flames licked the stick, then lit it in an amber blaze.

"Aren't you sore?" Georgie asked. "I am."

"I'm trying to ignore that," David said with a grin. The smile faded from his lips as he saw Mr. Hill entering a large tent.

"Georgie," David said, tossing another stick into the fire. "There is something I don't understand."

"What is it?" Georgie asked.

"If the California government outlawed slavery last year, why are you and your mother still with Mr. Hill?" David felt a little strange asking Georgie this question, but he really wanted to know.

"Because Mamma says we have nowhere else to go. We have no money," Georgie explained.

"When California becomes a state I'm sure that things will be different," David said.

Georgie sighed. "If it becomes a state," he said.

"Well, I guess we better sleep now," David said reluctantly as he stood up. "We'll be up tomorrow before the sun."

"Good night, David," Georgie said. "And thanks."

"For what?" David wanted to know.

"For being my friend," Georgie answered.

David went next to his father, who was already snoring softly. He tossed a blanket across a bed of pine needles and curled up under Celia's poncho. Despite the fact that he was tired, David couldn't drop off to sleep. Somewhere in the distance, a coyote howled. David shivered and pulled the scratchy woolen blanket up over his head and at last fell asleep.

FIVE DAYS LATER, on October 18, the group arrived in San Francisco. David's father had been right: the trip was tough. But all in all, these had been among the five best days in David's life. And now he was in San Francisco.

David was thrilled with the sights and sounds of the bustling city, and he had hundreds of questions for his father about San Francisco. Mr. Taylor told David that San Francisco was the most powerful and important city in California. It had sprung up practically overnight. Before gold had been discovered in 1848, San Francisco had had a population of about nine hundred people. Now, two years later, more than 20,000 people lived in the city alongside the beautiful San Francisco Bay.

David walked down the crowded streets, taking in the activity around him. He noticed that the main road through town was covered with wooden planks. But most of the others were dirt roads, muddy from a recent rain. There were no public sidewalks. David figured that the store-owners must be responsible for the walk in front of their buildings. Some had nice walkways, other buildings were fronted with muddy paths. David laughed out loud when he saw one building faced with a sidewalk made of old metal stovetops.

David and his father led their mules down to the waterfront. David saw that the muddy road was covered with bales of tobacco there. Men cracked their whips, urging on their horses and mules. Large boxes and barrels were hauled from storage buildings. They were swept along hand-to-hand and loaded onto pack mules. From there they would be taken to towns and mining camps like Spring Bar. Signs in store windows advertised silks from China, cigars from Cuba, oatmeal from Scotland. This busy city was a refreshing change from the isolated mining camp.

Boom!

David jumped, startled.

Boom! Boom!

From out in the harbor came the sounds of a cannon being fired. People began racing through the streets. "Watch out," David said, as someone pushed past him, nearly knocking him to the ground.

"It's a steamer!" someone shouted. "A side-wheel steamer is coming into the harbor!"

David joined the crowd racing down to the waterfront. All around him people were yelling. "It's the *Oregon*!" someone shouted.

David gazed out into San Francisco Bay. Never before

had he seen a more beautiful ship. She was flying what David thought must be one hundred American flags. Red, white, and blue streamers were draped all over the deck. Behind her hung a cloud of pale blue smoke from the recently fired cannon. And from the mast hung a huge sheet of canvas. David's heart soared when he saw the canvas. On it were printed the most amazing words:

CALIFORNIA ADMITTED!

Someone was ringing the ship's bell aboard the *Oregon*. People were playing musical instruments, singing, and shouting. As the steamer made her way into the bay, the other vessels saluted her by firing more guns.

"Hurray!" a young girl behind David shouted, waving a handkerchief. "California has been admitted into the Union. We are a free state!"

David shouted for joy. A free state, he thought. Now his family would remain in California.

He stood on his toes, craning his neck to get a better view, and spotted Georgie standing near the docks. Georgie put down the large box he was carrying, and wiped the sweat from his brow with his arm. Tex Ewell walked up behind Georgie, slapped his head, and forced him back to work.

A chill ran down David's spine. California was free. But what would become of Georgie Winston?

CHAPTER SEVEN
"The Plot"

"We're a state! California is admitted!" It was dusk when David arrived back at Spring Bar one week later. "California is admitted!" David shouted. "California is a free state!"

David had wanted to be the first to spread the news. As the expedition neared Spring Bar, he galloped his horse in front of the rest of the group.

The cool wind slapped at David's face as he raced through town shouting the news. Crowds of prospectors lined the dusty main street of Spring Bar. David tossed a copy of the newspaper *Alta California* to the crowd. People cheered and danced in the street when they learned the news.

David reached the Taylor Hotel, jumped off his horse and raced inside. "California is a state!" he cried in a hoarse voice. "A free state!" His mother and sister rushed out of the kitchen to greet him.

"That's wonderful!" David's mother said.

"And we were there to see it," David said. "The *Oregon* steamed into port with the news, and the town went wild. The city of San Francisco declared a holiday. The stores shut down, and everyone celebrated. It was incredible."

Just then, Mr. Taylor appeared in the doorway, a huge smile on his face. "That was nothing compared to the celebration we're going to have!" he said.

Mrs. Taylor ran into her husband's arms. "Welcome home," she said.

"It is our home," Mr. Taylor said. "It's our home—for good."

David and Celia laughed with joy.

DAVID'S PARENTS AGREED to let him and Celia stay up late that night. Everyone from the town had gathered in the saloon to celebrate.

Mrs. Taylor had tacked pieces of red, white, and blue cloth to the walls. David and Celia had painted a banner that read, "California: The 31st state."

Someone took out a fiddle and began playing a tune. Everyone joined in singing and clapping. Celia pulled David's arm. "Let's dance!" she cried.

"No," David said, pushing his sister's hand away.

"Come on, David," Celia pleaded.

"Well . . . okay," David said. "Just this once."

David and Celia whirled around on the dance floor. His

head was spinning with joy, his feet felt like they were dancing on clouds.

"I have to sit down," David huffed a while later. He let go of Celia, and wiped the sweat from his brow.

David and Celia dropped down on a bench. "Look how silly these people look," David said, shaking his head.

Since there weren't many women in the camp, some men tied bandannas around their arms and danced in the woman's place. David always laughed when he saw this.

"You looked just as silly a couple of minutes ago," Celia reminded him.

David stretched his legs. His muscles still ached a bit from his trip.

"No, sir, I don't like it," David heard a man say. "I don't like it one bit." David turned around. His eyes fell on Mr. Hill, who sat at a table with Tex Ewell.

"But what can you do about it, Mr. Hill?" Tex asked. "Sooner or later the law will catch up with us, and we'll be forced to release the slaves."

"Never," Mr. Hill said. "I need them. They are the ones who are making my mining business so lucrative."

"Let's dance again," Celia said.

"Not now," David said. "Listen." He nodded his head in Mr. Hill's direction.

"Well, I don't rightly see what we can do about it," Tex said, scratching his chin. "Not many folks round here own slaves in the first place. And most everyone else is happy that California is a free state."

"Most everyone else is a fool." Mr. Hill sneered.

"There's nothin' you can do about it," Tex said.

"Oh, yes, there is." Mr. Hill looked around and caught David's eye. Did he know that David was listening to him? Mr. Hill leaned in closer to Tex.

"Wait here!" David said to Celia. Mr. Hill had turned his back to David and Celia, making sure he could not be overheard. Before Celia could say a thing, David dropped to his hands and knees. He crawled under the long table, at the end of which sat Tex and Mr. Hill. As he approached the end, David slowed. He heard Mr. Hill's low voice over the sounds of the music, dancing, and laughter.

"I have it all figured out," Mr. Hill was saying. "Late tonight, we leave. I put out word that we're moving to a different camp. One of the southern mines. We'll head straight for Texas."

Texas? Why is Mr. Hill going to Texas? David wondered. Then it hit him. His heart raced as David realized the truth.

In Texas, Mr. Hill could keep his slaves.

AFTER THE LAST PERSON HAD LEFT THE SALOON, David sat alone on a cold wooden bench. The laughing, the singing, and the cheering still echoed in his ears. But there was a dark rumble there, too. A deep, dark, sinister rumble.

David stood up, and walked to the front door. A big harvest moon hung low in the western sky. How could Mr. Hill take Georgie away? There must be some way to stop him.

"Yes," David said out loud, "I will stop him."

"Stop who?"

David spun around. Celia was standing behind him.

"What are you doing up?" he asked. "It's late. The sun will be up soon. Mother will be angry if she catches us down here."

"I couldn't sleep, either," Celia said.

"Go back to bed, Celia," David said.

"Are you going upstairs, too?" Celia asked.

"In a few minutes," he said. "Goodnight, Celia."

"'Night, David."

There's nothing I can do, David thought to himself as Celia walked back up the stairs. But he knew he couldn't let Mr. Hill take Georgie away.

"I have to go to Mr. Hill's camp," David told himself. "I've got to warn Georgie."

CHAPTER EIGHT
"A Golden Friendship"

David quietly crept out of the hotel, lit his lantern, and set off down the road. He hoped he would be able to find his way to Mr. Hill's camp in the dark.

As he walked, a million thoughts raced through his mind. Had he heard Mr. Hill correctly? Was he really planning to take Georgie and the others away? And how would he, David Taylor, stop Mr. Hill? David looked up, searching the sky for an answer. The nighttime breeze whirred through the pine needles. The smoke from the lingering campfires drifted through the moonlight, making wispy gray lines that quickly disappeared. A streaking silver flash shot through the sky.

"A shooting star," David whispered. "Mother always said they bring luck. I hope she's right."

Finally, David reached the camp. He doused his lamp and peered through the branches. David saw Mr. Hill and a pair of his white workers loading the wagons. He looked around for signs of the slaves. He didn't see any. David swallowed hard. There was only one thing to do—confront Mr. Hill. David gathered his courage and stepped out of the trees into the clearing.

"Who's there?" Mr. Hill shouted.

"It's David Taylor, sir," David said, stepping out of the shadows and into the moonlight.

"What do you want, son?" Mr. Hill snapped.

"I kn-know what you're doing, sir," David stammered. "And the law says you can't. Your slaves are free now."

Mr. Hill laughed. "Son, you are sadly mistaken. Now kindly get off my property," he said, crossing to David.

"No, sir, I won't," David said.

"I said, *leave*!" Mr. Hill snapped as he pushed David to the ground.

"Leave my brother alone!" David looked up and saw Celia run out from behind a bush.

"I should have known you'd bring her along," Mr. Hill said.

"Celia!" David called. "Go home, now!"

Celia ran to her brother's side as Mr. Hill took a gun from his holster. "You children were warned," he snarled. "I am within my rights to shoot trespassers!"

Celia gasped.

"Not so fast, Hill," David heard a man say.

"I saw you leave, and figured you'd come here," Celia whispered in David's ear. "I brought Mr. Johnson—he'll help us."

Caleb Johnson stepped out of the shadows and slowly

approached Mr. Hill. "Now, Hill, put your gun away," he said. "We've just come here to talk to you."

David saw Hill's thin lips curve into a smile. But the knuckles on his hand stood out white against his trembling gun.

"I'm afraid there's been a misunderstanding, Johnson," Mr. Hill said.

"There's no misunderstanding," David yelled. "Let your slaves go!"

Hill chuckled.

"Well, now, that's just what they have done," he said. "My slaves have gone. Soon as they heard word that California was a free state, the fools hollered for joy and ran off into the woods. Good riddance, I say."

David looked at Celia. She looked at him, worry in her eyes. David bit his lower lip. Had he only imagined what Hill had said back at the dining hall?

Johnson nosed around the camp. "Looks like you're telling the truth, Hill," he said. David's heart fell. He couldn't believe that Georgie and his mother were gone.

"Of course I told the truth," Hill said, leaning back against his largest wagon. "I am a man of honor. All I ask is to be left in peace."

David gasped. The wagon!

In a flash, he remembered Georgie hiding under the bed of the wagon. David rushed to the wagon and climbed on it.

"Wait!" Hill shouted. "What do you think you're doing?"

Celia screamed as Hill pointed his gun at David.

"Don't do it, Hill!" Johnson called, pulling his gun and aiming it at Hill. David scrambled to the wagon's seat, leaned back, and threw up the false bottom of the wagon bed. He yelped—

There, packed tightly under the floor and gasping for breath, were five people—including Georgie's mother.

"You monster!" Celia screamed, rushing to Mr. Hill and pounding on him with her fists.

"He threatened to shoot us if we made a sound," Mrs. Winston gasped as David helped her and the others to their feet. "That's why we didn't dare to say a thing, even when we heard your voices."

"So they all ran away, did they?" Johnson asked Hill. "Good work, David!"

David wasn't listening. His heart fell as the last of the kidnapped people stood up. Georgie wasn't there.

"This here is my property," Mr. Hill shouted, waving his gun. "You are not gonna tell me what to do!"

"They are not your 'property,' Hill," Johnson said. "You know the law won't let you take these people out of the state. It's my job to enforce the law, and I will! You can take us to court, but I warn you, you won't win."

Mr. Hill's eyes darted back and forth. His gun was pointed at Johnson. David's heart raced. It was a standoff.

Ping!

Mr. Hill flinched, his free hand going to the back of his head, his face twisted with pain.

"What was that?!" he shouted, spinning around.

Caleb Johnson jumped forward and grabbed Mr. Hill by the neck. "I said put down the gun, Hill. Nice and easy." Johnson raised his gun to Mr. Hill's head and cocked the trigger.

Hill slowly lowered his gun. David breathed a sigh of relief.

"Take them all!" Mr. Hill shouted, waving his arms. "I've had enough with the law in this state. I'm heading back to Texas, where the law's on my side." He stormed off into the woods.

"David!" Georgie came running up to them, his slingshot in his hand. "I can't believe you came. How did you know Mr. Hill was going to kidnap us?"

"I overheard him talking to Tex," David said.

"You're a real hero," Georgie said.

David smiled. "No, Celia is. She's the one who brought the *alcade*. I just knew I couldn't let Mr. Hill take you away. I was so angry that I came here. I thought I could stop him by myself, but I was wrong."

"Georgie!" David saw Mrs. Winston running towards them.

"We're free, Mamma," Georgie said.

"Free, but what will we do?" Mrs. Winston said.

"Maybe this will help," Celia said. She lifted up her shirt to show the others a leather pouch tied around her waist. She took off the pouch and handed it to Georgie.

"What's that?" Mrs. Winston asked.

"Our gold," Georgie said, opening the pouch.

"Why are you carrying around the gold, Celia?" David asked.

"I'm the banker, remember?" Celia said. "And this is our bank." She pointed to the pouch.

"How can you have gold, Georgie?" Mrs. Winston said, frowning.

"We panned for it," Georgie explained, "just like everyone else."

"We can't accept it," Mrs. Winston said as she returned the pouch to Celia.

"What do you mean, you can't 'accept' it?" Celia asked. "It's Georgie's! He found most of it. And there's enough in there to get you started."

"And I promise to help us all find more," Georgie added.

A smile played across Mrs. Winston's lips. "Oh, Georgie," she said through tears, throwing her arms around her son.

"It's all right, Mamma," Georgie said as he smiled at David over his mother's shoulder. "This is the start of our life in California."

We will all stay in California, and live in freedom, David thought. He looked at the sky. The sun was beginning to rise, and its first rays glinted off the gold in Georgie's hand.

POSTSCRIPT

Miriam Matthews

Biddy Mason

Although the story of Georgie Winston is fiction, many enslaved African Americans were brought to California. One such woman was Biddy Mason, who was brought to California by a man named Robert Smith.

Smith took Biddy Mason and her three children to San Bernardino in 1851. They were treated as slaves, although by then California was a free state. Then, like Mr. Hill in the novel, Smith decided to move to Texas, taking his slaves with him. The sheriff of Los Angeles County stopped him from taking Mason and her children. Smith took the case to court. The judge ruled that Biddy Mason was no longer a slave, and that Smith could not take her and her family from the state against their will.

Biddy Mason went on to become a nurse. She used her earnings to buy land, which became very valuable. Mason became famous for her charity work. She died in 1891, one of the most respected citizens in Los Angeles.

More About . . .
The Compromise of 1850

As you read in the story, when California asked to join the United States as a free state in 1850 it started a great debate in Congress. At that time, there were thirty states in the United States. Fifteen were slave states, fifteen had outlawed slavery. The slave states feared that if a majority of states banned slavery, they might try to end slavery in *all* states. At first, the slave states refused to let California in the Union.

The debate in Congress was fierce. At one point, a senator from Mississippi pulled a gun and threatened to shoot another senator! At last, the senators agreed to compromise. *The Compromise of 1850*, as it was called, let California in as a free state. It also banned the slave trade in Washington, D.C., and let other territories vote on the slavery issue. In exchange, Congress passed a law called the Fugitive Slave Act. This law demanded that *all* people help catch runaway slaves. Slaves could no longer escape to free states and hope to be left in peace.

The Compromise of 1850 did not end the fight over slavery. It was only after the Civil War, which began in 1861, that slavery was ended in the United States.

"Gold!"

January 24, 1848, started out like any other day for James Marshall. Marshall, a carpenter, was building a sawmill for John Sutter near the south fork of the American River in the Coloma Valley. That morning, Marshall inspected a ditch his crew was digging. He later told a friend what happened:

> It was a clear, cold morning; I shall never forget that morning. As I was taking my usual walk, . . . my eye was caught with the glimpse of something shining in the bottom of the ditch. There was about a foot of water running then. I reached my hand down and picked it up; it made my heart thump, for I was certain it was gold.

California State Library

James Marshall

After scooping up the yellow flakes, Marshall put them in his hat and headed back to the logging camp. Marshall showed his boss, John Sutter, what he had found. The two men gave the yellow flakes to Jennie Wimmer, the only woman in the camp. She took the tiny bits of metal and dropped them into a boiling kettle of lye soap. Wimmer knew that if the strong soap could corrode the flakes, then they were not gold. When Wimmer poured the soap into a bowl to cool, the metal was unchanged. Marshall had found gold. The gold rush was on!

In The Hills

Upon hearing the news that gold had been found in California, thousands of people set out to seek their fortune there. When the first gold hunters arrived in San Francisco, housing was so scarce that abandoned ships were used as hotels and stores.

California State Library

Treasure hunters using a "Long Tom" in 1852

Treasure hunters did not stay in San Francisco, though. They headed to the hills and valleys, wherever there was a rumor of gold. Mining camps sprung up overnight. Here are some typical names: Humbug Canyon, Poverty Hill, Squabbletown, Chucklehead Diggings, Git Up and Git, Mad Ox Ravine, and Murderer's Bar.

Gold was found along the western slopes of the Sierra Nevada. The miners and prospectors used many methods to find the gold in the rivers and streams there. They used pans, rockers, and "Long Toms" (a large rocker eight to ten feet long). But no matter which method the miners used, searching for gold was a tough job. Few prospectors found gold on their first day out, or even their second. One woman miner wrote after her first day of panning:

> I wet my feet, tore my dress, spoilt a new pair of gloves, nearly froze my fingers, got an awful headache [and] took cold . . .

What was her reward? Gold dust worth three dollars and twenty-five cents!

California State Library

Ships in San Francisco Bay, 1851

The People

The gold rush caused the population of California to grow rapidly. In 1849, some twenty thousand people came to California by sea, and twenty-five thousand came overland. These "Forty-niners" were just the beginning. In 1850, forty-four thousand people came to California overland, and twenty-five thousand came by sea.

Chinese men came to San Francisco during the early years of the gold rush. They opened many stores in San Francisco and mining towns, but some sought their fortunes in gold. Mexicans came in large numbers, as did South Americans.

Searching for gold could be a very lonely life. Many people came to California with high hopes, only to leave with shattered dreams. Many others came to the state in search of gold, but stayed as farmers, carpenters, and shopkeepers. Some, though, were lucky enough to strike it rich. For them, the gold rush truly was the fulfillment of a "golden quest."

To Learn More About the Gold Rush

American Heritage Junior Library. *The California Gold Rush.* New York: Harper, 1961.

Blumberg, Rhoda. *The Great American Gold Rush.* New York: Bradbury Press, 1989.

Holliday, J.S. *The World Rushed In: The California Gold Rush Experience: An Eyewitness Account of a Nation Heading West.* Touchstone/Simon and Schuster: Englewood Cliffs, NJ, 1981.

Levy, JoAnn. *They Saw the Elephant: Women in the California Gold Rush.* Hamden, CT: Shoestring Press, 1990.

Seidman, Laurence, I. *The Fools of '49: The California Gold Rush 1848-1856.* New York: Alfred A. Knopf, 1976.